This SCRIBBLERS
book belongs to:

.......Shauna.......

For my very dear friend, Peggy, with much love.

ED

This edition published in Great Britain in MMXXI
by Scribblers, an imprint of
The Salariya Book Company Ltd
25 Marlborough Place,
Brighton BN1 1UB
www.salariya.com

SALARIYA
SCRIBO BOOK HOUSE SCRIBBLERS

© The Salariya Book Company Ltd MMXXI
Text © Elizabeth Dale MMXXI
Illustrations © Patrick Corrigan MMXXI

PB ISBN-13: 978-1-913337-16-2

1 3 5 7 9 8 6 4 2

A CIP catalogue record for this book is
available from the British Library.

Printed and bound in China.

Printed on paper from sustainable sources.

Visit
www.salariya.com
for our online catalogue and
free fun stuff.

BILLY
AND THE
BALLOONS

Written by
Elizabeth Dale

Illustrated by
Patrick Corrigan

SCRIBBLERS
a SALARIYA *imprint*

Billy's dad was magic with balloons. He turned them into dogs, giraffes, elephants... every shape you can imagine. Billy loved helping his dad sell them, especially on Christmas Eve. Everyone was so happy as they walked by with their Christmas trees and bags full of surprises.

'My fingers are almost too cold to hold the balloons,' said Billy's dad,
as the wind blew snow along the street.
'Let me hold them for you!' pleaded Billy.
'No, you're too tiny,' said his dad.
Billy frowned. He was always too tiny for everything!

Billy's mum brought them hot chocolate to warm them up.
'Super-duper!' cried Billy's dad, taking his mug.
Just then the wind blew harder, and the balloons bounced up and down – and out of
his hands! Oh no...

UP, UP, UP, THEY STARTED TO GO!

Billy ran and jumped... and just grabbed the strings.
'See! I *can* hold onto the balloons!' he cried. But then he
started to go up too!
'Come back, Billy!' called his mum.
'Hold on!' cried his dad.
And he ran and jumped... and grabbed Billy's foot.

But the wind blew harder, the balloons soared higher, and
Billy and his dad floated high over the roofs and trees.

When everyone noticed that just tiny Billy
Held all the balloons they were really scared SILLY!
'Oh Billy, hold tight to the strings!' they all cried,
So Billy held tight for a magical ride!

On and on they flew, over the school, over the farm and they just cleared the hill, but not the cow on the top.

'Come back, cow!' cried the farmer. And he ran and jumped... and grabbed the cow's foot.

And the wind blew harder and he started to go up, too.

But when the poor farmer saw just tiny Billy
Held all the balloons he was really scared SILLY!
'Oh Billy, hold tight to the strings!' the man cried,
So Billy held tight for a magical ride!

On they floated, above snowy trees and frozen lakes and over the nearby zoo.

The animals were amazed to see the farmer and his cow and Billy's dad and Billy and the balloons floating overhead.

The lions roared, the elephants trumpeted, and one baby monkey wanted to join in!

So he ran and jumped... and grabbed the farmer's foot.

'Come back, Baby!' the mummy monkey called, but he didn't want to!
So she ran and jumped... and grabbed her baby's foot.
But the wind blew harder, and she started to go up, too.

And when all the monkeys saw just tiny Billy
Held all the balloons they were really scared SILLY!
'Oh Billy, hold tight to the strings!' they all cried,
So Billy held tight for a magical ride!

As Billy waved goodbye to Santa and his reindeer, he had a great big smile on his face. Not just because he'd been flying through the sky with Santa Claus and the balloons, or because he'd helped save Christmas. Billy was smiling because of what Santa Claus had said.

It was BRILLIANT to be tiny!

When he'd finished, they flew to Billy's house with their final delivery – for Billy himself! 'Thank you, Santa,' said Billy.
'Thank you, Billy,' said Santa Claus. 'It was brilliant that you were tiny enough to help me. You saved Christmas!'
'It was great fun,' said Billy. 'Don't eat too many mince pies next year!'
'Don't worry, I won't!' Santa laughed.

And everywhere they went, Billy helped deliver Christmas presents. He was just perfect for squeezing down all the chimneys, tiptoeing into bedrooms and filling all the empty children's stockings.

They flew all over the world, over seas and mountains, lakes and forests.
It was amazing.

Suddenly Billy had a brilliant idea.

'I'm tiny, I won't be heavy on the sleigh with you,' he cried. 'I'll go down chimneys for you!'

'Will you?' asked Santa.

'I'd love to!' said Billy. 'It would be magic!'

Everyone held onto Billy's dad as he tied the balloons onto the sleigh.

Then he and the cow and the farmer and the monkey and his mummy let go. And off floated the balloons with the reindeer and the sleigh with Billy and Santa Claus on board.

So the mummy monkey caught hold of the nearest reindeer.
At last the poor tired reindeer could stop flying.

But the monkey and his mummy and the farmer and his cow
and Billy and his dad and the reindeer and Santa Claus full of
mince pies were all very heavy.

Too heavy for the balloons.

They all started to float down and down... until they landed on
the soft snowy meadow.

Everyone was very pleased – except for Billy and Santa Claus.

'What are you going to do about Christmas?' Billy asked him.

'I don't know,' Santa sighed. 'The balloons could fly just me
and my sleigh. But I'm too fat to fit down chimneys. I can't
deliver the children's presents.'

Billy frowned. Everyone would be so disappointed.

On and on they flew, over sparkly white meadows that loo[k]
though they were covered in delicious icing. Stars twinkled in the
above and Christmas lights sparkled in villages below.

Suddenly Billy heard a tinkling, jingling sound. It was Santa Claus and
his reindeer! But they were going very, very slowly.

'Can you give us a lift?' called Santa. 'My reindeer are tired out because
I've eaten too many mince pies and I'm far too heavy.'